#32
Eagle Rock Branch
5027 Caspar Avenue
Los Angeles, CA 90041

W9-BXY-875

GREAT MOMENTS IN OLYMPIC HISTORY

Olympic Swimming and Diving

Greg Kehm

rosen publishing's

rosen central

New York

Published in 2007 by The Rosen Publishing Group, Inc.
29 East 21st Street, New York, NY 10010

First Edition

Library of Congress Cataloging-in-Publication Data

Kehm, Greg.
  Olympic swimming and diving / Greg Kehm.
      p. cm. — (Great moments in Olympic history)
  Includes bibliographical references and index.
  ISBN-13: 9781-4042-0970-1
  ISBN-10: 1-4042-0970-0 (library binding)
  1. Swimming—History—Juvenile literature. 2. Diving—History—Juvenile literature.
3. Olympics—History—Juvenile literature. I. Title.
  GV836.4.K45 2007
  797.2'109-dc22

                                                          2006023339

Manufactured in the United States of America

On the cover: Olympic swimming champion Michael Phelps surges through the water in a 200-meter butterfly competition. At the 2004 Athens Olympics, Phelps racked up an amazing 8 medals: 6 gold and 2 bronze.

CONTENTS

CHAPTER 1

Origins of Swimming and Diving

Swimming is one of the oldest human activities. In ancient times, it was a recreational pastime that was considered good for one's health and was also often included in military training. In Egypt, prehistoric cave paintings show figures doing what appears to be the breaststroke or dog paddle. Other ancient Egyptian art shows swimmers practicing what may be the front crawl. An ancient tomb in Greece shows swimming and diving scenes from about 2,500 years ago. Art from the ancient Middle East, Italy, and Mexico also features swimming scenes. Written references to swimming can be found in many ancient texts.

The ancient Greeks did not include swimming in the Olympic Games held between the eighth and fourth centuries B.C. However, it was an important part of education for young men, and swimming pools were common. Swimming was part of the training for warriors in ancient Japan. Historical records show that the first swimming races were held in Japan as early as 36 B.C.

During the Middle Ages in Europe, knights were expected to know how to swim in their heavy metal armor. By the end of the Middle Ages, the common practice of swimming without clothing became less popular since it was not considered acceptable behavior by religious leaders. A German professor, Nicolas Wynman, wrote the first known book about swimming in 1538. It included tips for learning the breaststroke.

Competitive Swimming

It wasn't until the early 1800s that swimming began to be a widely practiced sport. Competitive swimming began in 1837 with the creation of the National Swimming Society of Great Britain, an association that organized races in the six swimming pools that had been built in London. Most swimmers competed using the preferred stroke of the day—the breaststroke.

Amanda Beard of the United States plows ahead to capture a gold medal in the 200-meter breaststroke final at the 2004 Athens games. Beard made her Olympic debut in Atlanta in 1996 where, at the tender age of 14, her impressive breaststroke earned her one gold and two silver medals.

5

The Front Crawl

In 1844, a small revolution occurred at a London swimming meet. Competing in the races were some Native Americans. While the British swimmers swam the breaststroke, the Native Americans surged ahead using an unusually fast style of swimming, in which their legs kicked up and down and their arms moved like "windmills." It was with great ease that Native Americans Flying Gull and Tobacco placed first and second. Yet the British weren't impressed. The splashing produced by the Native Americans' form of the front crawl was seen as savage to British gentlemen, who liked to keep their heads above water. As a result, British swimmers continued to stick to the breaststroke and the newly developed sidestroke, which had emerged in the mid-1800s.

In the 1870s, however, the front crawl was reintroduced to England—this time by an Englishman named J. Arthur Trudgeon. Trudgeon was a swimming coach who traveled to South America and was impressed by the overhand stroke that native people used to move quickly through lakes and rivers. When Trudgeon returned to Great Britain, he began teaching the stroke, which became known as the "trudgeon." It was similar to the front crawl we know today, but with a scissor kick, rather than the flutter kick now used. Meanwhile, in the 1880s, Frederick Cavill, an English swimmer who had settled in Australia, witnessed young men from the South Sea Islands using a flutter kick with the crawl. In fact, the native people of the Americas, West Africa, and some Pacific islands had been using this stroke for thousands of years. Cavill taught his sons the stroke, and they soon began to break records with it in competition. The stroke gained worldwide fame as the Australian crawl. In the 1950s, it became known simply as the front crawl.

Lisbeth Lenton at the 2004 Olympics.

Origins of Diving

Diving was originally a way for people to entertain themselves—and others—by jumping off cliffs and rocks into water. Particularly thrilling and dangerous were high dives in which divers flew gracefully through the air before disappearing into water. Early travelers to Mexico and Hawaii were fascinated by the amazing and courageous dives performed by native people who plunged from the high cliffs into coastal waters.

As a competitive sport, diving emerged in Europe at the beginning of the nineteenth century. At the time, a dive was a simple plunge into water similar to that used by swimmers. The goal of the diver was to travel as far as possible under water. Early divers competed by plunging into ponds. Later, they dove from platforms into swimming pools.

However, the sport of diving as we know it today has much more in common with gymnastics than with swimming. Many modern divers have training as gymnasts. It is not surprising that the type of competitive diving performed at the Olympics evolved from gymnastics. In the 1700s,

Many divers come from a gymnastics background. Before becoming one of the sport's most impressive young stars, Australia's Matthew Mitcham was a world mini-trampoline champion.

Scandinavian and German gymnasts began practicing their routines by landing in the water instead of on hard floors. In the summertime, gymnastics equipment was taken to beaches where gymnasts could perform acrobatics from platforms and land in the ocean. Gymnasts performed acrobatic movements, such as somersaults and twists, before plunging into the water. Soon, these routines were considered a separate sport. To distinguish this sport from plain diving, or plunging, diving with somersaults or twists was called fancy diving. Until the early twentieth century, separate competitions were held for plain and fancy diving.

In Europe, platform diving first took place on temporary structures attached to ladders that were set up outdoors. These early platforms were not very sturdy and often frightened divers by shaking back and forth in strong winds. As diving developed later in North America, divers leapt from springboards instead of platforms. The first springboards were planks of wood covered with coconut fibers so that divers wouldn't slip and fall.

South African diving champion Jenna Dryer seems as if she's spinning out of control, but every move is precisely rehearsed and timed. At 18, Dryer competed at the 2004 Athens Olympics, reaching the finals in the 3-meter springboard event.

Swimming and Diving at the Olympics

Swimming and diving competitions were quite popular when the first modern Olympic Games were held in 1896. Only men competed in these Olympic Games, which included three swimming events. An 18-year-old Hungarian named Alfréd Hajós won two gold medals.

It wasn't until the 1904 Olympic Games held in St. Louis, Missouri, that diving became an Olympic sport. Women's platform diving was introduced in the 1912 Olympics. One of the earliest diving champions was a tiny young American named Aileen Riggin. She won her first gold medal at the 1920 Olympics in Antwerp, Belgium, in the first women's Olympic springboard event. Riggin was only 14 and weighed just 65 pounds (29.5 kg) at the time.

In the 1920s and 1930s, one of the world's great swimmers was an American named Johnny Weissmuller. Winner of five Olympic medals, Weissmuller never lost a race. He was only one in a long series of American swimmers who dominated the sport throughout the century. Swimmers such as Helene Madison, Don Schollander, and Debbie Meyer helped to establish the United States as a leading competitor in Olympic swimming. Madison won three gold medals in 1932. Schollander was the first man to win four gold medals for swimming in 1964. Meyer was the first swimmer to win three individual gold medals in 1968. At the 1972

Olympics in Munich, Germany, Mark Spitz became known as the "greatest swimmer of all time" by winning seven gold medals. Following in Spitz's footsteps was 19-year-old Michael Phelps, who took home eight medals—six gold and two bronze—at the 2004 Olympics in Athens, Greece. The United States also produced two of the century's greatest divers: Patricia McCormick and Greg Louganis. Each of them took great risks to win gold medals in both springboard and platform diving events.

This 1967 photograph shows five top American swimmers of the day, among them Debbie Meyer (second from left) and Mark Spitz (second from right). The following year in Mexico, Meyer would be the first swimmer to win three individual gold medals at a single games and Spitz would take home the first four out of eleven Olympic career medals.

Of course, talented athletes from other countries have consistently challenged, and often upset, American champions at the Olympic Games. In the late twentieth century, Russia was a tough competitor due to their fast-as-lightning sprinter, Aleksandr Popov. Australia, with 22,831 miles (36,735 km) of coastline, also produced some outstanding swimmers, such as record-breaking Dawn Fraser. Since the early 1990s, China has become one of the world's greatest diving nations, a title earned in part by the outstanding performances of one of its brightest stars, Fu Mingxia.

Some of the most unforgettable moments in Olympic diving and swimming have involved athletes from countries with little or no tradition of victory in the pool or on diving boards. Divers such as Italy's Klaus Dibiasi and swimmers such as the Netherlands' Hendrika "Rie" Mastenbroek and Suriname's Anthony Nesty have brought great pride to their homelands. Their triumphs have kept the rest of the world believing that with lots of talent, hard work, and a little bit of luck, the Olympic dream is always within reach.

CHAPTER 2

The Early Years (1896–1936)

The first modern Olympics took place in the games' birthplace of Athens, Greece, in the summer of 1896. Since these games were not well-publicized internationally, athletes were not selected to be on national teams. Instead, they came as individuals and had to pay all their own costs. Some contestants were tourists who just happened to be in the area during the games. Approximately 240 male athletes from fourteen countries competed in the Olympics, which featured three swimming events: the 100-meter, 500-meter, and 1,200-meter freestyle races. In freestyle races, swimmers used the stroke of their choice. Since it allowed for more speed, most swimmers chose the front crawl.

The First Olympic Swimming Champion

The first ever Olympic swimming champion was Alfréd Hajós of Hungary. Born in the Hungarian capital of Budapest, Alfréd vowed to become a great swimmer at the age of 13, after his father drowned in the Danube River. Five years later at the Athens games, Hajós captured two gold medals in the 100-meter and 1,200-meter freestyle races. He had hoped to win the 500-meter race as well, but because the race came immediately after the 100-meter and right before the 1,200-meter, it was impossible for him to compete in it.

Hajós's victory was even more impressive considering the environment in which the swimming events took place. They were not held in a swimming pool. Instead, competitors jumped off the side of a boat into the Mediterranean Sea and swam to shore. Confronted with 12-foot (3.7-m) waves and icy waters of 50°F (10°C), Hajós was more concerned with battling the elements than beating his opponents. In fact, prior to the 1,200-meter race, Hajós tried to keep his body warm by covering it with a thick layer of grease. He soon found that this method didn't work. After the race, Hajós explained his victory by declaring, "My will to live completely overcame my desire to win."

Making Rules

During the first few Olympics, competitive swimming wasn't very organized. One problem, which certainly affected Alfréd Hajós, was the lack of a controlled swimming environment. At the 1900 Paris Olympics, swimmers raced in the Seine River. During the 1904 St. Louis games, they competed in a small lake.

Furthermore, there were no universally accepted regulations governing the sport. The early Olympic Games featured some events that may sound odd today. The 1896 Athens Olympics included a 100-meter race in which only Greek sailors could compete. At the Paris Olympic Games in 1900, swimmers participated in obstacle races and underwater races. The latter proved to be unpopular since spectators couldn't see the swimmers. At the 1904 Olympic Games in St. Louis, Missouri, swimmers competed in a "plunge for distance" race. After doing a standing dive into the water, they had to glide forward—without swimming, pushed along only by the force of the dive—for 1 minute or until their heads broke the surface of the water. High-diving events were also featured at the 1904 Olympics for the first time. Divers jumped not from a platform or springboard, but from a "springless" board.

With an increase in international competitions, a universal set of rules was needed. Prior to the 1908 London Olympics, leaders of the eight participating countries—Britain, France, Germany, Belgium, Hungary, Denmark, Sweden, and Finland—met in the British capital to create the International Swimming Federation (FINA). The 1908 Olympics were the first in which swimming was regulated. It was also the first time that swimmers competed in a specially built 100-meter swimming pool. To this day, FINA sets down globally accepted rules for swimming and diving competitions. Aside from recording world records, FINA also regulates Olympic swimming and diving.

Olympic Women

Women were first allowed to compete in Olympic swimming and diving events at the 1912 games held in Stockholm, Sweden. However, many people still believed it wasn't proper for women to participate alongside men. In 1920, fourteen women qualified for the U.S. Olympic team. The performances of these young women erased any doubts that they weren't as athletically gifted as the men.

The youngest and smallest among this determined group was an American swimmer and diver named Aileen Riggin. Born in Newport, Rhode Island, she barely survived the flu as a child.

In 1928, 4 years after having retired from her Olympic career, Aileen Riggin gets ready to make a backward flip dive off the springboard at a London swimming pool.

15

To build up her strength, she joined a girls' swim team and also studied ballet. Riggin was just 14 when she arrived at the Olympic Games in Antwerp, Belgium. She was only 4 feet 7 inches (1.4 m) tall and weighed a mere 65 pounds (29.5 kg).

Belgium was still recovering from the destruction of World War I (1914–1918) and was quite poor. Swimming and diving programs were held in a muddy canal filled with cold water. The stress of competing in the springboard diving event was the least of Riggin's worries. As she later explained, "I had another mental block. It was about sticking in the mud at the bottom. . . . I kept thinking, the water is black and nobody could find me if I really got stuck down there. And if I were coming down with force, I might go up to my elbows and I'd be stuck permanently, and nobody would miss me and I'd die a horrible drowning death."

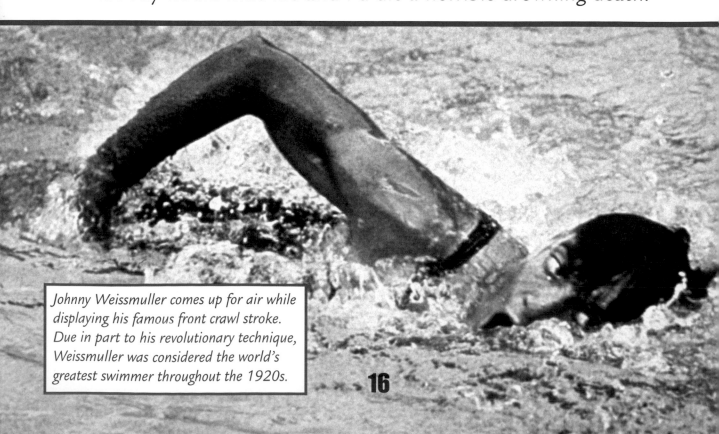

Johnny Weissmuller comes up for air while displaying his famous front crawl stroke. Due in part to his revolutionary technique, Weissmuller was considered the world's greatest swimmer throughout the 1920s.

Despite her fears, Riggin won a gold medal in the 1920 Olympics, making her America's smallest and youngest gold medalist ever. Four years later, Riggin returned to the Olympics in Paris, a little older and a little taller. She won a silver medal in springboard diving and a bronze medal for the 100-meter back-stroke. In doing so, she became the first person—and to this date, the only woman—to win medals in both swimming and diving.

Tarzan in the Pool

Also competing at the 1924 Paris Olympics was a handsome young swimmer from the United States named Johnny Weissmuller. One of the greatest swimmers of all time, Weissmuller had grown up swimming along the shores of Lake Michigan in Chicago, Illinois. Over time, he developed a revolutionary front crawl that made him impossible to beat. This was certainly the case at the Olympic Games in Paris, where he won gold medals in the 100-meter and 400-meter freestyle and was a member of the winning relay team for the 4x200-meter freestyle race.

Actually, Weissmuller almost didn't make it to the Olympics. As a member of the U.S. team, he needed an American passport to travel. However, Weissmuller—who had been born in what is today Romania—was not officially an American citizen. With time running out, the swimmer ended up switching birth certificates with his American-born younger brother and was issued a passport just in time.

At the 1928 Olympic Games held in Amsterdam, the Netherlands, Weissmuller once again captured gold medals in both the 100-meter freestyle and 4x200-meter freestyle relay events. His good looks and endless winning streak turned him into a celebrity. In 1932, Hollywood invited him to audition for the lead role in a film called *Tarzan the Ape Man*. By then, Weissmuller had set sixty-seven world records and had never lost a race. He was chosen over 150 other candidates for the role of Tarzan. He retired from swimming and went on to become the most famous Tarzan of all time.

Johnny Weissmuller

The Chocolate Race

The 1936 Olympics in Berlin, Germany, are often remembered for the presence of Nazi dictator Adolf Hitler watching from the stands. Another event that stood out in the 1936 Olympics was the triumphant victory of African American athlete Jesse Owens, who won international fame for being the first American to win four gold medals in track-and-field events at the Olympics. However, equally memorable were the dramatic gold medal wins by 17-year-old Dutch swimmer Hendrika "Rie" Mastenbroek.

Over 5 days, Rie Mastenbroek competed in four events. In each of them, she came from behind her opponents at the last minute to score unexpected victories. In the 100-meter freestyle event, she was in fifth place at the halfway point and third place when she was just 10 meters from the finish. Victory seemed out of reach until, in a sudden burst of energy, she shot past her opponents to capture her first gold medal. In the 100-meter backstroke, all seemed lost when Mastenbroek got tangled up in one of the lane ropes. Nonetheless, she kept a clear head and sprinted ahead to earn a silver medal. In the 4x100-meter freestyle relay, the Dutch were lagging behind the first-place German team. As the final swimmer on the Dutch relay team, Mastenbroek was behind her German opponent. Then, with only 20 meters to go, Mastenbroek raced to the finish, scoring a second gold medal.

However, Mastenbroek's most dramatic victory occurred in the 400-meter freestyle race. Prior to the event, top Danish swimmer Ragnhild Hveger had shared a box of chocolates with all the swimmers except Mastenbroek. Feeling snubbed, Mastenbroek vowed she would seek her revenge in the pool. And she did. In the very last moments of the race, only 25 meters from the finish, she pulled ahead of Hveger and beat her opponent by 1 meter, earning a third gold medal and the title of the top female swimmer in the world. Revenge proved sweeter than chocolate. With her string of last-minute victories, Rie Mastenbroek became the first woman to win four medals at a single Olympics.

CHAPTER 3

After the War (1948—1968)

During World War II (1939–1945), the Olympics were canceled. When they resumed in 1948, a new stroke was introduced into swimming events. In the 1940s, competitors who swam the breaststroke discovered that they could move more quickly by bringing both arms over their heads at the same time and moving their legs together in what was called the dolphin fishtail kick. This vigorous new style was soon banned for those competing in breaststroke events. However, under the name "butterfly," it later became a competitive stroke in its own right. Meanwhile, diving increased in popularity, particularly in the United States, with the arrival of a bold and daring young female diver.

Diving for Gold

Thousands of young Olympic hopefuls dreamed of qualifying for the 1948 Olympic Games in London. Among them was Patricia McCormick, a 17-year-old diver from California. McCormick was incredibly disappointed when she didn't make the U.S. diving team—especially since she missed her chance by less than 0.1 point. Instead of giving up, she set her sights on winning a gold medal at the 1952 Olympic Games in Helsinki, Finland.

As it turned out, McCormick underestimated her abilities. In Helsinki, she won two gold medals: one for springboard diving and one for platform diving. At the time, her signature dive—a $1\frac{1}{2}$ twist with a somersault—was considered exceptionally

After winning a gold medal for the women's springboard competition at the 1952 Olympics in Helsinki, American diver Patricia McCormick receives congratulations from silver medalist Madeleine Moreau (left) of France and bronze medalist Zoe Ann Olsen (right) of the United States.

A triumphantly grinning Dawn Fraser of Australia shows off the gold medal she won for the 100-meter freestyle competition during the 1960 Olympics in Rome.

Don made his sister promise to keep training. Around the same time, Fraser left school to work in a dress factory and earn money. When she could, she continued training at a local pool. One day, swim coach Harry Gallagher spotted her and thought she had talent. In fact, he was so impressed that he coached Fraser for free, convinced she had the potential to compete in the Olympics. Fraser made it to the 1956 Olympic Games in Melbourne, Australia. She won her first individual medal in the 100-meter freestyle event. She also shared a gold medal with team members in the 4x100-meter freestyle relay. She went on to win a second gold for the 100-meter freestyle at the 1960 Olympic Games in Rome, Italy.

Italy's King of the Board

Just as Dawn Fraser ignited Australians' pride in swimming, Klaus Dibiasi inspired Italians' passion for diving. Dibiasi was only 17 in 1964 when he participated in his first Olympics in

Italian diving hero Klaus Dibiasi executes a perfect dive during the 10-meter platform event at the 1972 Munich games. For his winning performance, Dibiasi earned the second of three consecutive Olympic gold medals for platform diving.

25

Tokyo. His father and coach, Carlo Dibiasi, had competed as a diver in the 1936 games. Klaus surprised everyone when he won a silver medal in platform diving at the Tokyo games. Italian fans went wild. It was the first time an Italian had won a medal in a diving event.

When Dibiasi returned to his hometown of Bolzano, Italy, he was a star. With the support of the people in his town, Dibiasi continued to train hard for the 1968 Olympic Games. When he competed in platform diving in the 1968, 1972, and 1976 Olympics, he took gold medals every time. For his third and last gold medal, however, Dibiasi had to work harder than ever. He was competing against Greg Louganis, a rising star in the sport of diving from the United States. By this time, Dibiasi was 29 years old, making it more difficult for him to defeat a younger, talented diver. However, Dibiasi beat Louganis by more than 23 points. Dibiassi set a record as the first diver to win three gold medals for the same event and to win medals at four Olympic Games in a row.

In Sickness and in Health

In 1960, the sport that most interested 13-year-old Michael Jay Burton, the son of an Iowa truck driver, was cross-country running. One day when he was out riding his bicycle, however, Michael was hit head-on by a truck. The damage was serious.

He severed tendons under his right knee and the ball joint of his hip was forced into his rib cage. Doctors said he would never be able to compete in sports again. However, they recommended that Burton swim to strengthen his leg muscles.

Burton trained hard at swimming. His dedication to swimming over a period of 7 years earned him a place on the 1968 U.S. Olympic team. He traveled with the team to Mexico City, Mexico, for the Olympic Games. The day before the qualifying heats for the 400-meter freestyle, Burton woke up feeling sick. Later, he fainted in an elevator. Even though he felt weak and dizzy, he qualified for the event and went on to win the gold medal. Three days later, he won the 1,500-meter freestyle by 18.4 seconds—a victory margin that has yet to be matched for that event.

Four years later, at the 1972 games in Munich, Germany, Burton once more showed his strength by making one of the biggest comeback performances of the Olympic Games. Juggling a full-time job and a family had left Burton with little time to train. As a result, he barely made it to the finals of the Olympic trials. Once there, he qualified as a member of the U.S. team by a slim margin. Most people didn't think that he would be able to win the 1,500-meter race like he did in 1968. Burton lagged behind in second place for the first 1,200 meters of the race. However, with less than 300 meters to go, Burton surged ahead to the finish and won the third gold medal of his career!

CHAPTER 4

The Great Ones (1972–1988)

Mike Burton's surprising comeback victory wasn't the only Olympic feat that people were talking about during the 1972 Olympic Games. In Munich, swimming fans had the thrill of witnessing one of the greatest athletic performances in Olympic history. The hero of this Olympics was a 22-year-old Jewish American swimmer from California named Mark Spitz. Known for his speed, agility, and winning butterfly stroke, Spitz not only fulfilled all the pregame hype that surrounded him, but surpassed it, becoming one of the greatest swimming "superstars" of all time.

The World's Greatest Swimmer

Mark Spitz was a natural-born swimmer. He was only 2 years old when his father taught him to swim. By the age of 8, he was swimming competitively. By his tenth birthday, Spitz held a world record and had been named the world's best swimmer in the 10-and-under age group.

As a teenager, Spitz continued to impress onlookers with his talents. He awed spectators with his effortless technique and speed, particularly when he swam the butterfly. The butterfly stroke, one of the most difficult strokes to swim, was Spitz's specialty. When Spitz traveled to the 1968 Olympics, he boldly predicted that he would earn six gold medals. Spitz won two gold medals, but in

American swimming phenomenon Mark Spitz plows through the water at the 1972 Munich games, where he made Olympic history by capturing seven gold medals, the most won by any athlete for any sport at a single games. His performance turned him into an overnight superstar in the United States.

team freestyle relays. In individual events, he won a silver and a bronze medal. Such a result would have been a triumph for most athletes, but Spitz was very disappointed with himself. He vowed to dedicate himself to training harder than ever.

At the 1972 games in Munich, his efforts paid off. He surpassed the predictions he had made 4 years earlier. This time, he went on to win

Mark Spitz smiles victoriously from the center of the winner's podium after accepting his gold medal for the 100-meter butterfly at the Munich Olympics. Following the games, posters featuring Spitz wearing his gold medals sold out across North America.

an astonishing seven gold medals, each time setting a new world record. To this day, no other Olympian in any sport has matched such a feat. By the end of the Olympic Games, Spitz was known as the greatest swimmer of all time.

Going the Distance

Mike Burton was famous for his short-distance sprints. Mark Spitz earned his "greatest" title by excelling at different strokes that he swam at various distances. However, when it came to the

Standing Ovation

Like most swimming fans around the world, Vladimir Salnikov was greatly disappointed when the Soviet Union boycotted the Los Angeles Olympics in 1984. He thought the 1984 Olympics would be his last opportunity to win a gold medal. After 4 years of hard training, he was crushed that he wouldn't be able to compete. Vladimir's wife, Marina—a former track-and-field athlete and sports training psychologist—became his coach that same year. With her encouragement, Salnikov began training for the 1988 Olympics. By the time the 1988 Olympic Games began in Seoul, South Korea, 8 years had gone by since his last Olympic performance. Although Salnikov was only 28, he was considered "over the hill" for a competitive swimmer. For this reason, he was not favored to win. Early in the 1,500-meter freestyle, Salnikov struggled to keep up with two German opponents. However, he was able to eventually pass his rivals and take the lead. In a spectacular comeback, he won the gold medal. Salnikov set a record for becoming the oldest Olympic swimming champion in 56 years.

Perhaps more emotional than Salnikov's win was the reaction of his peers. On the evening of his triumph, Salnikov went to the Athletes' Village for a late-night snack. To his surprise, he received a standing ovation from 250 athletes and coaches in the cafeteria. No other athlete in Seoul received such heartfelt congratulations.

determination and endurance required for the long haul, one of the greatest distance freestylers was a Soviet swimmer named Vladimir Salnikov.

The son of a sea captain in Leningrad (now known as St. Petersburg), Salnikov began swimming at the age of 8. When he was 16, he competed at the 1976 Olympics in Montreal, Canada. Salnikov only took fifth place in the 1,500-meter freestyle, but was the first Soviet swimmer to make it to the Olympic finals. Things were different 4 years later when the Olympics were held in the Soviet capital of Moscow. Cheered on by a roaring crowd of Soviet supporters, Salnikov succeeded in doing what long-distance swimmers had been dreaming of for years. He swam the 1,500-meter freestyle in under 15 minutes and won a gold medal for his efforts. Salnikov then went on to win two more gold medals—one in the 4x200-meter freestyle relay and another one in the 400-meter freestyle!

The Length of a Fingernail

One of the most unexpected events in Olympic history took place at the 1988 Olympics in Seoul. Matt Biondi of the United States was favored to win the 100-meter butterfly competition. Biondi had already won a gold medal as a member of the 4x100-meter freestyle relay team at the 1984 Olympics and won a bronze medal in the 200-meter freestyle event in Seoul.

However, during the 100-meter butterfly race in Seoul, Biondi found himself head-to-head with Anthony Nesty of Suriname. Suriname is a small South American country bordered by Guyana, French Guyana, and Brazil. Nesty had also competed in the 1984 Olympics but had placed twenty-first in the 100-meter butterfly. Both athletes were undoubtedly surprised when, in the last meter of the race, Nesty pulled ahead to win the gold medal. Nesty won the race by a split second: 53.00 seconds to Biondi's 53.01

When Suriname's homegrown swimming talent Anthony Nesty won the country's first and only Olympic gold medal, the government honored the event on stamps and gold and silver coins.

seconds. Biondi was a gracious loser who said, "One one-hundredth of a second—what if I had grown my fingernails longer?"

Nesty's surprising win was a victory for his country as well as himself. Aside from being the first black athlete to win an Olympic gold medal in swimming, Nesty was also the first Olympic champion from the tiny South American nation of Suriname. Biondi

American swimmer Matt Biondi punches the air in triumph after winning the 50-meter freestyle event at the 1988 Olympics in Seoul.

decided to work harder to win his other Olympic events. He competed in five more events and won gold medals in all of them. Furthermore, in four out of the five events, he set new world records. The incredible number of medals he picked up at the Seoul games—a total of seven—tied him with Mark Spitz for having won the most swimming medals in a single Olympics.

The World's Greatest Diver

When Klaus Dibiasi won his last Olympic gold medal in Montreal, Canada, he had to work hard to beat Greg Louganis of the United States. Louganis was already a tough competitor in the world of diving at the age of 16. Before earning a spot on the United States Olympic Diving Team, Louganis had to overcome many obstacles. Born in California to teenage parents of Samoan and Swedish ancestory, he was given up for adoption and raised by a Greek American family in San Diego, California. As a child, Louganis was teased for his ethnic background, his dyslexia, and the fact that he preferred activities such as acrobatics, dance, and gymnastics to baseball and football. At home, however, Louganis's father was impressed when he saw his son doing gymnastic flips off the diving board into the family pool. He enrolled Greg in diving classes. Just 2 years after his first class, 11-year-old Louganis scored a perfect 10.00 at the 1971 U.S. Junior Olympics. Hard work and classical dance training gave his diving performance a smooth elegance and precision rarely seen in the sport of diving.

During a troubled adolescence that included problems with depression and drugs, Louganis eventually turned to diving as a way to cope with his problems. He was successful as a diver, which made him feel good about himself. He also enjoyed the solitude of the long daily training sessions. Although Louganis won the silver medal for platform diving at the 1976 Olympics, he was disappointed with his sixth-place finish in the springboard diving event. Louganis's dreams of winning diving events in the 1980 Olympics were shattered when the United States boycotted the games. He would have to wait another 4 years before he could compete for the Olympic gold. Louganis decided to work harder to prepare for the 1984 Olympic Games in Los Angeles, California. His hard work paid off. He won gold medals in both the platform diving and springboard diving events. His impressive score of 710.9 points in the platform event was, and still is, the highest ever recorded.

Louganis hoped to repeat his performance at the 1988 games in Seoul. But this time, victory didn't come so easily. While competing in the next-to-last qualifying dive for the springboard event, Louganis attempted a tricky reverse $2\frac{1}{2}$ somersault in pike position. His jump off the board wasn't strong enough. He hit his head on the board and fell into the water. Fellow athletes and spectators were terrified that Louganis might have been badly hurt.

In fact, Louganis's scalp wound was so serious that he required stitches. Yet, with only one more dive required to qualify, he wouldn't give up. A half hour after having his scalp temporarily sewn up, he was back on the board. He only agreed to go to the hospital the following day, after he had successfully

Louganis is shown here getting out of the water after hitting his head on the diving board. When he finally agreed to go to the hospital after qualifying for the springboard event, he had to have 5 stitiches.

qualified to compete. The day after, he was back and in perfect form. He performed eleven dives and won his first gold medal.

In the last round of platform diving, Louganis was three points behind 14-year-old Xiong Ni of China. Faced with the most difficult dive in his program, Louganis expertly executed a perfect reverse $3\frac{1}{2}$ somersault. He won the gold medal by 1.14 points. His stunning victories made him the second athlete to win gold medals in both springboard and platform diving in two Olympics. Patricia McCormick had been the first. His victories also earned him some of the highest scores ever achieved in an international diving competition and the title of the "greatest diver of all time."

Greg Louganis is still considered one of the best divers ever. Aside from artistry and athleticism, he exhibited great courage when he announced to the world in 1995 that he was HIV positive.

CHAPTER 5

New Millennium, New Records (1992–2004)

The end of the last millennium and the beginning of the new one witnessed an explosion in the popularity of aquatic sports. This in turn led to a variety of exciting new events. It is not surprising that at the Olympics, swimming and diving tickets sell faster than those for many of the other sports. At the 1984 Olympics in Los Angeles, California, synchronized swimming for women made its first appearance as a competitive event. At the 2000 Olympic Games in Sydney, Australia, synchronized diving was introduced. In this sport, a pair of divers perform the same dive at the same time. In the meantime, a new generation of talented athletes are training to set new world records.

Little "Miss Perpetual Motion"

American swimmer Janet Evans was swimming laps when she was only 2 years old. It is no wonder that she grew up to be the world's top long-distance female swimmer. Although Evans grew up, she always remained small and light. Her schoolmates teased her about her size. However, it didn't stop her from breaking three world records in 1987—the 400-meter, 800-meter, and 1,500-meter freestyle events. What she lacked in size—her height was 5 feet 4 inches (1.6 m) and she weighed 99 pounds (45 kg)—she made up for with her unbeatable "windmill in a hurricane" stroke and trademark bursts of speed. This technique allowed her to defeat opponents with much longer arms and legs and earned her the nickname "Miss Perpetual Motion." Evans was 17 when she participated in the 1988 Olympics. She won three gold medals and the hearts of millions of Americans.

By the time she entered the Olympic Games in Barcelona, Spain, in 1992, Evans had been winning 400-meter races for 6 years. However, in the final lap of the race, she lost to Dagmar Hase of Germany, who beat her by a mere 30 centimeters. Evans was stunned, but resolved to do even better in her next event. Two days later, she won the 800-meter race by 8 meters, becoming the first woman to capture four gold medals in swimming. Although Evans retired from swimming after competing in the 1996 Olympic Games, her world records for the 800-meter and 1,500-meter races remain unbroken.

The "Queen of Diving"

In 1991, China's Fu Mingxia was only 12 when she became platform diving champion of the world! However, her hopes of competing in Olympic diving events were almost taken away by a new regulation. The International Swimming Federation (FINA) made a rule that said divers in international competitions must turn 14 the end of the year in which the competition is held. Fortunately for Fu, she would turn 14 in 1992.

Fu headed to the 1992 Olympic Games in Barcelona shortly before her fourteenth birthday. She won her first gold medal and became the youngest Olympic platform champion. As a former gymnast, Fu amazed spectators and fellow divers by tackling incredibly difficult

One-Second Art

"It takes a diver only 1.7 seconds to go from the 10-meter platform to the water surface down below," said Fu Mingxia. "So I call it a 1-second art. It requires you to fully display the beauty of the sport in only a second. It's very demanding, but I love the challenge."

40

dives with great ease. Fu remained unbeatable going into the 1996 Olympic Games. Now a 17-year-old who was 2 inches (5 cm) taller and 30 pounds (17 kg) heavier, Fu once again made history by winning gold medals in both platform and springboard events. By then, she was known as the "Queen of Diving" and had set a high standard for a new generation of Chinese divers.

However, 7 years of training had exhausted Fu. She retired from diving, enrolled at a Chinese university, and tried to lead a normal life. Yet as the 2000 Olympic Games approached, Fu couldn't resist the temptation to compete once again. Fu only had 6 months to train for the synchronized diving event with her partner, Guo Jingling. First, Fu won a silver medal with Jingling in springboard synchronized diving. Then she came back to win her fourth gold medal in an individual springboard diving event, making her the first Olympic diver to win five medals.

The Russian Rocket

Another unforgettable performance in the 1996 Atlanta Olympic Games was by a young sprinter named Aleksandr Popov. He was called the "Russian Rocket" because he had a habit of starting out slow and then racing ahead to pass his opponents at the last minute.

In the 1996 Olympics, Popov was swimming far behind his opponent Gary Hall Jr. during the 100-meter freestyle event.

Then, only 15 meters from the finish, Popov swam his fastest to get ahead of his rival and win the gold medal. Three days later, he repeated the same performance in the 50-meter freestyle event. Only a few strokes away from the finish, Popov once again swept past first-place Hall to win the fourth Olympic gold medal of his career.

Rising Star

Another great swimmer—Michael Phelps—made a name for himself at the 2000 Olympics as the youngest American male swimmer to compete in the Olympics since 1932. Less than a year later, he became the youngest man to break a world record in the 200-meter butterfly event. Phelps, also known as the "Baltimore Bullet," was only 19 when he won eight medals—six gold and two bronze—at the 2004 Olympics. He joined legend Mark Spitz as the only swimmer to win four individual gold medals in one Olympics. The comparisons with Spitz didn't end there. Like Spitz, Phelps had an amazing ability for excelling at a wide range of strokes and distances. Phelps beat Japan's Takashi Yamamoto in the 200-meter butterfly. An hour later, he swam the first leg of the 4x200-meter freestyle relay and helped bring the United States a gold medal victory over Australia.

Today, like other Olympians, Phelps is looking ahead to the future. "I want to be known as one of the greatest swimmers of all time and take swimming to a new level," Phelps said in a 2005 interview. "My aim is to do even more in the future, because who knows what is possible?"

New and Improved Technology

Swimming and diving have come a long way since they first appeared at the Olympics over 100 years ago. Today's swimming pools are temperature controlled: they must be exactly 79°F (26°C). State-of-the-art pools feature gutters that "swallow" waves and plastic lane markers that reduce water turbulence. Touch pads at the end of each lane precisely record swimmers' times and send them electronically to timing systems. Swimsuit designers use supercomputers to design ultrathin fabrics that are like second skins. They hug the swimmer's body to reduce friction and water absorption, which can improve a swimmer's time.

Because, humans are mammals who spend their lives on land, the talented swimmers and divers who glide like fish through water or soar like birds through the air capture our imaginations. Their feats thrill us because they seem magical. Ultimately, it is this magic, even more than the medals, that makes watching the Olympics so irresistible.

American swimming champion Michael Phelps celebrates after winning a gold medal at the Athens games.

43

Timeline

1896 First modern Olympic Games are held in Athens, Greece. Alfréd Hajós of Hungary wins two gold medals and becomes the first Olympic swimming champion.

1900 Swimming competitions at the Paris, France, games take place in the Seine River.

1904 Swimming competitions at the St. Louis, Missouri, games take place in a lake. High diving is introduced.

1908 The International Swimming Federation (FINA) is formed and establishes the first globally accepted rules for swimming and diving. Olympic swimming events are held in a swimming pool for the first time at the London, England, games. Springboard and platform diving events are introduced.

1912 First women's Olympic swimming and diving events held at the Stockholm, Sweden, games.

1920 U.S. diver Aileen Riggin wins a gold medal in springboard diving at the Antwerp, Belgium, games. She becomes America's youngest and smallest gold medalist ever.

1924 At the Paris, France, games, Riggin becomes the first person to win medals in both swimming and diving. U.S. swimmer Johnny Weissmuller captures his first two gold medals.

1936 In Berlin, Germany, the Netherlands' Hendrika "Rie" Mastenbroek is the first women to win four medals at a single Olympics.

1948 The first Olympics after World War II (1939–1945) are held in London, England. The butterfly stroke is introduced.

1952 American diver Patricia McCormick picks up gold medals for springboard and platform diving at the Summer Olympics in Helsinki, Finland. Breaststroke is accepted as a separate stroke with its own event.

1964 At the Summer Olympics in Tokyo, Japan, Dawn Fraser becomes the first women to win four gold medals. Klaus Dibiasi wins a silver medal in platform diving, becoming the first Italian to win a diving medal.

1968 Dibiasi wins a gold medal in platform diving at the Mexico City, Mexico, games. Swimmer Michael Burton wins two gold medals. Swimmer Mark Spitz wins four medals, including two gold medals in team events.

1972 Dibiasi wins his second gold medal in platform diving at the games in Munich, Germany. In a great comeback, Mike Burton wins his third gold medal. Spitz sets an Olympic record with seven gold medals and seven world records—a feat no other Olympian has accomplished.

1976 Dibiasi wins his third gold medal in platform diving at the Montreal, Canada, games. He beats American Greg Louganis, who takes home the silver. Soviet swimmer Vladimir Salnikov makes his debut.

1980 Salnikov wins three gold medals at the games in Moscow, USSR.

1984 Louganis wins gold medals in platform and springboard diving, with a record score for platform at the games in Los Angeles, California.

1988 Salnikov wins his fourth gold medal at the games in Seoul, South Korea. Louganis again wins two gold medals. Anthony Nesty of Suriname becomes the first black athlete to win an Olympic swimming medal. Swimmer Mark Biondi wins seven medals. Swimmer Janet Evans wins three gold medals.

1992 Evans wins her fourth gold medal at the games in Barcelona, Spain. Alexander Popov wins two gold medals.

1996 Popov repeats his double gold medal–winning performance at the games in Atlanta, Georgia.

2004 Michael Phelps makes Olympic history at the games in Athens, Greece, becoming the first American to win eight medals at one Olympics.

Glossary

backstroke A stroke in which the swimmer lies on their back, performing a flutter kick and rotating the arms alternately backward.

boycott An organized refusal to take part in something as a form of protest.

breaststroke A stroke in which the swimmer lies on their stomach and moves their arms forward and outward from the chest while the legs kick in a froglike manner.

butterfly A stroke in which both arms are lifted together out of the water and flung forward, in combination with the dolphin kick (in which both legs are held together).

dyslexia A learning disability that involves problems with reading, writing, and spelling. A person with dyslexia may see and write letters and numbers backwards.

fancy diving The name used for competitive diving in the early twentieth century. It developed from exercises performed by gymnasts over water.

flutter kick A kick, usually performed with the front crawl, in which legs are held straight and move up and down alternately.

freestyle A swimming event in which competitors can use any stroke they choose.

front crawl The fastest of all swimming strokes. Alternate arm movements, accompanied by a flutter kick, move a swimmer forward.

gutter A trench along each side of a swimming pool used to catch and carry off excess water created by waves.

platform diving An event in which a diver dives from a fixed, unbending diving surface. In Olympic competitions, the platform is 10 meters above the swimming pool.

relay A race between teams of swimmers in which each swimmer on a team completes one part of the total distance.

scissor kick A kick used to push a swimmer forward in which the legs move like the blades of a pair of scissors.

sidestroke A swimming stroke performed by a swimmer on their side in which arms are swept separately towards the feet while the legs do a scissor kick.

springboard A flexible diving board that can be adjusted to create more or less "spring." In Olympic competitions, the springboard is 3 meters above the swimming pool.

tendon A strip or band of tough white fiber connecting a muscle to another body part, such as a bone.

touch pad The pad at the end of each swimming pool lane that a swimmer touches to register their time. The pad sends an electronic signal to the timing system.

For More Information

Canadian Olympic Committee
21 St. Clair Avenue E., Suite 900
Toronto, ON
Canada, M4T 1L9
(416) 962-0262
Website: http://www.olympic.ca

International Swimming Federation (FINA)
Avenue de l'Avant-Poste No. 4
1005 Lausanne
Switzerland
41-21-310-47-10
Website: http://www.fina.org

International Swimming Hall of Fame (ISHOF)
One Hall of Fame Drive
Fort Lauderdale, FL 33316
(954) 462-6536
Website: http://www.ishof.org

Swimming Canada National Office
Suite 700, 2197 Riverside Drive
Ottawa, ON
Canada K1H 7X3
(613) 260-1348
Website: http://www.swimming.ca

U.S. Olympic Training Center–Colorado Springs
National Headquarters
1 Olympic Plaza
Colorado Springs, CO 80909
(719) 632-5551
Website: http://www.usolympicteam.com

USA Swimming
1 Olympic Plaza
Colorado Springs, CO 80909-5707
(719) 866-4578
Website: http://www.usaswimming.org

World Olympians Association
Regional Office of the Americas
The Biltmore
1200 Anastasia Avenue, Suite 140
Miami, FL 33134
(305) 446-6440
Website: http://www.woaolympians.com

Web Sites

Due to the changing nature of Internet links, the Rosen Publishing Group, Inc., has developed an online list of Web sites related to the subject of this book. This site is updated regularly. Please use this link to access the list: **http://www.rosenlinks.com/gmoh/swim**

For Further Reading

DK Publishing. *Olympics*. New York: DK Children, 2005.

Fischer, David. *The Encyclopedia of the Summer Olympics*. London, United Kingdom: Watts Publishing, 2004.

Fox, Virginia. *Swimming*. Farmington Hills, MI: Lucent Books, 2003.

Gonsalves, Kelly A., and Susan Lamondia. *First to the Wall: 100 Years of Olympic Swimming*. East Longmeadow, MA: FreeStyle Publications, 1999.

Greenberg, Doreen, and Michael Greenberg. *Fast Lane to Victory: The Story of Jenny Thompson*. Terre Haute, IN: Wish Publishing, 2001.

Mullen, P. H. *Gold in the Water: The True Story of Ordinary Men and Their Extraordinary Dream of Olympic Glory*. New York: St. Martin's Griffin, 2003.

Bibliography

Amateur Athletic Foundation of Los Angeles (AAFLA). "An Olympian's Oral History: Patricia McCormick" and "An Olympian's Oral History: Aileen Riggin Soule." Retrieved February 2006 (http://www.aafla.org/6oic/OralHistory/OHmccormick.indd.pdf; http://www.aafla.org/6oic/OralHistory/OHriggin.indd.pdf.).

Flatter, Ron. "Louganis Never Lost Drive to Dive." *ESPN.com*. Retrieved February 2006 (http://espn.go.com/sportscentury/features/00016086.html).

Great Britain Diving Federation. "History of Diving." Retrieved February 2006 (http://www.diving-gbdf.com/history.php).

International Olympic Committee. "Sports: Aquatics, Olympic Sport Since 1896." Retrieved January 2006 (http://www.olympic.org/uk/sports/programme/index_uk.asp?SportCode=AQ).

International Swimming Federation (FINA). "Swimming" and "Diving." Retrieved February 2006 (http://www.fina.org/).

International Swimming Hall of Fame (ISHOF). "Honorees: Swimmers and Divers." Retrieved February 2006 (http://www.ishof.org/).

Michael Phelps. "Home Page." Retrieved February 2006 (http://www.michaelphelps.com/2004/index.html).

Roberts, M. B. "Spitz Lived Up to Enormous Expectations." Top North American Athletes of the Century. *ESPN.com*. Retrieved February 2006 (http://espn.go.com/sportscentury/athletes.html).

Sports Illustrated for Women. "100 Greatest Female Athletes." Retrieved February 2006 (http://sportsillustrated.cnn.com/siforwomen/top_100/21/ [Dawn Fraser]; http://sportsillustrated.cnn.com/siforwomen/top_100/29/ [Janet Evans]; http://sportsillustrated.cnn.com/siforwomen/top_100/80/ [Aileen Riggin Soule]; http://sportsillustrated.cnn.com/siforwomen/top_100/92/ [Fu Mingxia]).

Sports Potential, Inc. "Swimming." Retrieved February 2006 (http://www.sportspotential.com/cgi-bin/results/sport.cgi?fileId=1472&sportId=530).

United States Olympic Team. "Summer Sport Athlete Bios." Retrieved February 2006 (http://www.usolympicteam.com/19.htm).

Index

About the Author

Like current U.S. swimming star Michael Phelps, Greg Kehm hails from Baltimore, Maryland, where he graduated with a BA degree in English from Towson University. A freelance writer and journalist, Kehm has also been an avid swimmer (his favorite stroke is the front crawl) and die-hard Olympic fan since he was a teenager.

Photo Credits

Cover, p. 43 © Al Bello/Getty Images; pp. 5, 6 © Adam Pretty/Getty Images; p. 7 © Mike Hewitt/Getty Images; p. 8 © Kristian Dowling/Getty Images; p. 10 © Express Newpapers/Getty Images; p. 15 © Hewerdine/London Express/Getty Images; pp. 16, 31 © Getty Images; p. 18 © Keystone Features/Getty Images; p. 21 © Keystone/Getty Images; pp. 23, 25, 30 © Staff/AFP/Getty Images; p. 24 © AFP/AFP/Getty Images; pp. 29, 33, 37 © Tony Duffy/Allsport; p. 34 © Simon Bruty/Staff/Getty Images; p. 36 © Pascal Rondeau/Getty Images; p. 40 © Ross Kinnaird/Allsport.

Designer: Daniel Hosek
Editor: Colleen Adams